For Becca, the best dog in the universe, and
those who help rescue animals of all kinds—
may they find their nests and fur-ever homes!
—MG

To Francisco with all of my love.
—LU

little bee books

An imprint of Bonnier Publishing USA
251 Park Avenue South, New York, NY 10010
Text copyright © 2018 by Maria Gianferrari
Illustrations copyright © 2018 by Luisa Uribe
Little Bee Books is a trademark of Bonnier Publishing USA, and
associated colophon is a trademark of Bonnier Publishing USA.
Manufactured in China HUH 0618
First Edition
2 4 6 8 10 9 7 5 3 1

Library of Congress Cataloging-in-Publication Data
Names: Gianferrari, Maria, author. | Uribe, Luisa, illustrator.
Title: Operation Rescue Dog / by Maria Gianferrari; illustrated by Luisa Uribe.
Description: First edition. | New York, NY: Little Bee Books, [2018] Summary: At the
same time seven-year-old Alma, lonely and desperately missing her mother, decides
to rescue a dog as a surprise for Mami's return, a scared pup named Lulu is
rescued by volunteers from the side of the highway and is eagerly
awaiting a place to call home. Identifiers: LCCN 2017057227 | Subjects: |
CYAC: Rescue dogs—Fiction. | Dogs—Fiction. | Hispanic Americans—Fiction.
Classification: LCC PZ7.G339028 Op 2018 | DDC [E]—dc23
LC record available at https://lccn.loc.gov/2017057227

ISBN 978-1-4998-0667-0
littlebeebooks.com
bonnierpublishingusa.com

OPERATION
RESCUE DOG

by Maria Gianferrari   illustrated by Luisa Uribe

little bee books

Alma wears Mami's scarf like a hug.
Her mami is far away
in a place called Iraq.
Alma hasn't heard Mami's voice
since her seventh birthday,
three long months ago.
They write letters
with spaces between them
as far away as the moon.

A half-moon glows on Lulu's chest.
For weeks, Lulu slept under the moon.
Dumped near a highway,
eating acorns,
drinking from mud puddles,
smelling shadows,
freckled with ticks.

Did Lulu howl at the moon
to hear her own voice?

The tangy scent of
arepas de queso
fills the kitchen.
Abuela stirs huevos.
A rescue dog was Alma's idea.
One the color of Mami's eyes,
a surprise friend for Mami's return.
Alma packs some snacks.
It's a long, long journey
to the Operation Rescue Dog truck stop.

In a parking lot far from Alma's home,
Lulu waits with rescuers
for the Operation Rescue Dog truck.
Lulu squeezes between legs.
Her tail points down.
The air smells . . . uncertain.
Where is she going?

Alma rubs Mami's scarf on her cheek.
The fleece feels almost like a kiss.

Can a dog feel like a hug?

Lulu cowers.
The rescue truck arrives.
Joe, the driver, wipes his brow.
His daughter, Mary, stretches her legs.
They have already driven many miles
north to south.
Now they will journey northeast
to help dogs find new homes.

Trees blur.
Fields fly by.
The sun sleeps behind a cloud.
Alma tastes the words of
her favorite book on her tongue.
The one Mami read to her,
the one she will read to her new friend.
On her lap sits a yellow leash.
Mami's favorite color.

Lulu's tail is tucked
as she's led onto the truck.
Dogs bark, yelp, bay.
Lulu shivers and shakes.

Thump. Click. Click.
Whoosh goes the air from the tire.
Abuela eases the car onto the grass.
No other cars pass.

Lulu's curled in a crate.
Yowls echo.
Wind whistles.
The truck's floor hums.
Lulu sniffs the air.
It smells like . . . fear.

Abuela paces on the phone.
Alma plucks dandelions.
The air smells like rain.
The blue car must wait.

Doors squeal open
for a walk break.
Dogs whimper and yip.
Corn tassels whisper in the wind,
their stalks like a forest.
Brakes of a passing bus screech—
Lulu lurches.
Into the corn forest
Lulu runs.

Rain pummels.
Lightning flashes.
Thunder clashes.
The blue car can only wait.

Voices call her name,
but Lulu hides
in corn shadows,
smelling green,
musty earth
instead of fear.

Sniff. Sniff.
A new smell . . . ham.
Mary makes a sandwich trail.
Lulu drools,
inches forward,
and shares Mary's sandwich.

The rescue truck rolls
down the highway.
On Mary's lap,
nose in the wind,
smells like . . . joy.

The tow truck arrives.
A donut's a funny name for a tire.
Alma can finally laugh.
A rainbow arcs.

Alma breathes in honeysuckle air
and studies the photo:
a lolling tongue, shining eyes,
half-moon rising on her chest.
Honeysuckle smells like . . . hope:
a dog named Lulu.

Lulu's ears flap in the wind
as the rescue truck rolls into the lot.
Lulu's tail thumps—
Everything smells . . . new.

Alma and Abuela arrive.
The Operation Rescue Dog stop
pulses with voices and color and song.
It smells like . . . Christmas.
Alma's yellow leash waits,
as bright as the sun.

"Lulu!" sings Alma.
Lulu sniffs Alma's hand
and gobbles a biscuit.

Lulu licks Alma's cheek;
Alma rubs Lulu's belly.

Lulu's new leash smells like . . .
family.

Abuela is smiling
and shaking Joe's hand.
Alma is laughing
and hugging Mary.
Lulu is leaping
into the car.

Alma smells like . . . home.
So does Lulu.

Hola Mami,

... vimos con Lulu y
... arque

AUTHOR'S NOTE

Our dog, Becca, a dixie chick from Chattanooga, Tennessee, is a rescue dog. Becca was found in an empty lot adjacent to a highway, a spot known for dumping unwanted dogs. Shy and covered with ticks, Becca was lured into a car with some leftover chicken by her namesake rescuer, Rebecca, and her husband, Ross. We are forever grateful that they took her in and brought her to a local dog rescuer, Debbie Ginn at For the Love of Dogs, instead of a shelter where she would have had only hours before being euthanized. Like Lulu, Becca journeyed on a transport truck with stops along the way. We met her in New Hampshire and took her to her forever home, then in Massachusetts. For the Love of Dogs, and its partner shelter, Mutts 4 Rescue, are only two of countless dog rescue operations that transport dogs from high-kill Southern shelters northward to no-kill shelters, foster homes, or, if both people and dogs are lucky, their forever homes.

So many healthy, homeless dogs (and cats) die needless deaths. The statistics are startling: More than seven animals are killed every minute in the United States—more than 9,000 animals a day! Many, but not nearly enough, are rescued by the tireless work of dedicated volunteers—from those who temporarily foster dogs until homes can be found, to those who drive the transport vans, trucks, even airplanes, to those receiving dogs on the other end for fostering and/or adopting.

There's a friend out there just waiting for you: the most loyal, loving companion. When you're ready for a dog (or cat or even a rat, for that matter), please consider adopting from your local shelter or an online rescue operation such as petfinder.com, rather than contacting a breeder. If it's a specific breed you want, there are tons of rescue organizations focused on particular breeds. You will reap the rewards of rescuing a pet. There is a saying in the pet rescue world: Who rescued *who*? Indeed! It may not be grammatically correct, but it's all heart.

For more information on pet rescue, please visit the following websites:
• AllPaws: allpaws.com
• American Society for the Prevention of Cruelty to Animals (ASPCA): aspca.org
• Best Friends Animal Society: bestfriends.org
• Hope for Paws: hopeforpaws.org
• Petfinder: petfinder.com

If you can't adopt a dog or other pet, here are some other ways you can help:
• Volunteer to walk, groom, play with, and help socialize dogs, cats, or other creatures at your local animal shelter
• Volunteer to help clean kennels and cages
• Organize a fund drive: rather than birthday or holiday presents, consider asking family members and friends if they'd like to make a donation to a local shelter
• Stage a blanket or bed drive
• Donate food, treats, or other supplies
• Sponsor a shelter pet
• Spread the word about pet adoption
• Educate family, friends, neighbors, and acquaintances about the importance of spaying and neutering their pets

A portion of the proceeds from this book will be donated to Best Friends Animal Society in Kanab, Utah, the largest no-kill animal sanctuary in the United States. Not only does Best Friends shelter dogs and cats, but also horses, parrots, bunnies, pigs, and even some wild creatures.

Glossary of Spanish Words

abuela	grandmother	**de**	of
Alma	a girl's name meaning *soul*	**huevos**	eggs
arepas	corn pancakes	**Mami**	Mommy
arroz	rice	**queso**	cheese
café	coffee